Despite facing numerous challenges and adversities over the years, Pearl has exhibited remarkable resilience. As the eldest among ten siblings, growing up in a large family was a daunting experience. However, Pearl's determination remained unwavering. The author has endured nerve-racking mental health issues, medical concerns, and immense stress, yet her passion for writing has never diminished. She refuses to surrender or succumb to obstacles, facing them head-on with an indomitable spirit and an unyielding resolve to persevere.

Hi

Best Wishes to the reader and a lovely Peaceful World Hugs from

Pearl Marie Murdoch

x

P.S. you Can always Use this book to hold a Table up.

Pearl Marie Murdoch

SHORT STORY COLLECTION

AUSTIN MACAULEY PUBLISHERS™

LONDON • CAMBRIDGE • NEW YORK • SHARJAH

A CIP catalogue record for this title is available from the British Library.

ISBN 9781035817726 (Paperback)
ISBN 9781035817733 (ePub e-book)

www.austinmacauley.com

First Published 2024
Austin Macauley Publishers Ltd®
1 Canada Square
Canary Wharf
London
E14 5AA

I would like to thank Austin Macauley Publishers for all the hard work.

My mum Alice Murdoch and dad Angus Murdoch, for without their help I could not have done this. My sisters and brothers for all the stories and all my friends.

Thank you.

Table of Contents

Beautiful Wales

You took me in, sweet Daffodil, flowers
Growing in the Welsh meadows
With your long trumpet-shaped center.
Your lovely Scent, and Colour, of Lemon and
Primrose yellow.
and grey-green basil leaves.
blowing in my ears with your beautiful
Welsh voices. I had to come to you.

Meadow Croft Hotel, Colwyn Bay where I
used to work.
Waiting on Tables, serving Leek and Potato Soup
That tasted superb.
Red Tablecloths, White Aprons, starched.
Green Napkins to wipe away the Gravy
from hungry mouths, from a 3-course meal.
With Welsh cakes for afters from the oven
Hot and tired from overuse.

Seagulls flying overhead on my day
off, waiting for me to give them my attention
As I take in the Colwyn salty sea air
and clear my head from work.

Llandudno only down the road,
Taking driving lessons to there
from a Teacher with no Patience for me at all.
I enjoyed to put my foot down you see
who could blame him, for feeling Scared,
I'm sorry, if you're still there.

A Gentle Giant was my friend
I wonder, where you are today
I make my way up the road, back
to work, to Tidy my room, and write
Home letters,
to brothers and sisters I had left behind,
who I couldn't forget, even if I tried.

Oh, Beautiful Wales, who helped me out,
How could I ever forget your
lovely Face?
So when I see a Daffodil
my heart beats for you
but at your Pace.
how much I have to learn.

A Black Hole I Am In

Chapter 1

Cold eating into my tired weary bones I make my way down to the pit the snow has turned to ice, my boots can't grip. I slip, and scream out, no one hears me. I sit exhausted for what seems like hours. But it's only minutes. Please God! I shout, I don't know how I can go on. Give me strength please give me strength to get back up again! I rest for a short while.

Then I find some strength from within and get back up. It seems that my maker listened to me! As I knew he would. I coughed up blood last week in church.

No one noticed as I hid my hankie, the hymns went ahead, so did the Sermon, the Vicar gave, about how lucky we miners were. Lucky to be able to provide for our families, ha, half the workers' money went back to the Bosses. And the local pub owned by them. The shop you get food put on the slate. The Bosses had it so. Your wages went back to them. No wonder we got fed up. Morale was down. I felt old at 29 years of age. The average age for a miner was 30. Alice, my wife, was losing weight. Trying her best. Looking after the children was a full-time job. Cooking over the fire made with wood and anything that would burn. My boots would help keep us all warm. But I had no money for new ones.

The slate mine is grueling back breaking work, with no let up. The men that work beside me are like brothers, we all share the same dangerous conditions down the pit. The same landscape, families that have grown up, gone to church together, in our beautiful Country of Wales. We all sing hymns that lift the heart, shame songs don't fill the belly.

I Put On My Lipstick

I put the old lipstick on, it's called Sunrise.
Brown eyeshadow, on my saggy eyes
when I look in the mirror, I see lots of lines
I try not to worry
But I want to cry

I once was a young girl
Pretty and proud
Now I am an old girl
With my head in the clouds
Yet I still surviving
Thanks, to all the problems I've had

I cope the best I can,
I suppose I am not too bad
For 93, even with pains in my knees
So I smile at my reflection
and head through the door
Here I come, are you ready for more?

A Beautiful Brother

You were my friend, Douglas
Who listened, who cared.
I'll never forget you or your beautiful red hair
Your cheeky smile when I told you off.

Your kindness towards me when you'd slip me a few Bob.
I'm sorry that you've gone.
I miss you every single day!
But listen! to me Brother
I'll love you till my dying breath
So, you get some rest now
From the cruelty of this world
And when we meet again
I'll hug you,
And I'll look after you in your world.

I Was A Dunce At School

I was never very clever.
I wore a Dunces Hat.
I used to stand in the Corner
Having to watch, my back, as the kids
Threw pens and splattered ink at me.
The teacher was a bully, letting me go through that.
And boy, did she go on, and on, and on
Never letting me have a minute to get
my breath back, as she rattled on and on
I think she hated our class

I couldn't read and write,
I found it all, so hard,
But maybe it's because,
Getting hit with sticks by dad drove me to
depression. I often felt quite blue,
I knew I didn't deserve that.
Nor do any of you.

But when I look back,
It wasn't all so bad,
I'm pretty strong, and it's taught me
I can fight back.

Here We Are Sunday School

10 to 3 ticks the yellow plastic clock on the kitchen wall. And faded wallpaper, brown with age, we put our best clothes on, bought second hand from Great Homer Streets Paddy Market, Liverpool. We make our way to Bethany Hall Dinas Lane. We sit on benches uncomfortable hard but made of oak. Dark rich and beautiful. The lady teachers all wear pastel-coloured hats of green, blue, and pink. They're beautiful. The men wear suits that are pressed to perfection, highly polished shoes, shirts ironed crisply and different coloured ties, that tighten when they reach the high notes of the hymns. Sometimes we all sing out of tune, to the Organ that needs a rest, and has long run out of life. As I feel now, old, and tired. We get in groups, and listen to Sunday School Teachers telling stories of Jesus, and how it's better to be good than bad. My beautiful leather red Bible earned with questions, answered by myself on different stories and passages of Jesus. The lovely gold leaf pages I flick over, trying to understand, sometimes I find hard to understand it all.

Dad comes home from work, nearly always angry. Mum often cries. There's a lot to get me down, not much food to feed us all, 10 in all. I'm oldest. Christmas a knock comes on the door. The Head Sunday School Teacher, Mr Elliot has brought the biggest food hamper I've ever seen, all from his and other Sunday School Teachers pockets. I'm 59 today, how could I ever forget them. Why would I forget the helping hands that were good to us children. It's Jesus who got me through it all.

And the kindness of Mrs Bell with her soft and lovely kind face gone but not forgotten. Dot who has been through so much herself with breast cancer. Jim the top man who never ever gave up on anyone.

Thank you.

Dad

In another world

Dad, sitting in the chair, at the nursing home, 5 minutes from Mum who sits at home watching films on Telly.

Listen Dad, we love you, and we love Mum but none of us could cope, I'm sorry it's come to this.

But hey Dad, the Girls are great, and we can take you out and we take you home once a week, to sit with Mum, in your lovely garden. It breaks my heart, when I see you, down, I wish you were well because, I don't want you to feel sad, or hurt. We'll always be there for you. I go home feeling depressed, but Dad wc all love you please understand. I feel upset when I leave you there, we love you, Dad.

My Old Lipstick

I put on the old Lipstick, It's called Raspberry Sunrise.
Brown eyeshadow put on quickly,
on my sagging blue eyes.
I brush my Red, fading hair.
And take a backward glance
before I head out the door to the dance.

I see a face filled with worry,
I've lines like a map, on my cheeks!
I keep up to date with fashion,
But it's done nowt for my full figure. And double chin.

I once was a young Girl
Pretty and proud
Now I'm an old girl
With my head in the clouds
Yet, I'm still surviving the best
That I can, so world here I come.
Thanks for all the problems
I cope the best I try
And I danced all night.
I'm not giving up just yet.

Rainbow

A Rainbow sent from Heaven
Appears in the sky magnificent
Yellow, red and orange, green, mauve and blue,
My oh, my oh, my
What a lovely sight you make.

You give me hope, when
Ever, I feel low, Isn't that great?
You lift me up when I
Look up to you, with your beauty and
your lovely colours smiling
Smiling down, to cheer me up
letting me know, it's okay to cry.
Whenever I see a Rainbow
Remember God is near,
Or so I am told

I give cheer for you,
Because you make me smile.
As I wipe my ears.
I know it will be okay.

I Love You Mum

Mum is drinking too much Julie and I'm afraid she'll have another fall. Last time she broke her collar bone. Well Pearl, that what men do to you.

It's the terrible hard life mum's had, but that brandy's too strong, Julie. Ha, Ha, how does she do it, and still keep the house nice, and still cope? I don't know, it's been a horrible time.

I laugh, but it's not funny, not funny at all, 79 is not that old today.

Mum is a survivor, losing her mum to TB when she was 15, maybe the brandy helps with the pain she feels, Julie.

She has had 10 children, I'm the oldest, 1 brother left. 3 dead.

Just wish mum would eat a bit more, she's lost so much weight.

Yes I do worry.

Lately I've been worried about myself too. A spell in hospital Bell's Palsy they thought I'd had a stroke.

No it was brought on through worry.

Douglas's death at 54 Fatty Liver. They say through the drink.

I say Douglas drank, because he was upset about his divorce, being told he couldn't have children, A high rise flat. Getting beaten up in the lift of the flats.

Losing Rory our brother of 21 to suicide by car fumes, that was a lot for one to cope with. Douglas was the world to me, and I miss him every single day. To watch him drink himself to death, made me ill. He wouldn't listen to anyone, we all tried out best. Dougy my wee brother gone at 54, Glen 48. Back to mum, we went to Llandudno for 5 days on Shearing Coaches, mum and Julie and I. Had a well-earned rest, thanks to the hard work of the staff at the Marina Hotel on the Llandudno Sea front. The beautiful well-cooked meals and the lovely people of Wales, who made the holiday everything it should be. Mum ate everything.

We put, Julie and I, Douglas and Glen in Llandudno Sea. The ashes that is, Douglas James would have wanted that because he liked Wales. Had many, many happy memories there, Glen also R.I.P. As for Mum, Julie and I will do our bit, as she did for us all growing up. We have to do our bit too.

It's all been so sad 3 brothers gone, 2 through drink Glen and Dougy, Rory suicide.

I'm the eldest, it's all been so hard, but we'll get by. We have to.

Beautiful Wales I Miss You So

You took me in, oh Daffodil
with your lovely scent and colour.
Blowing in the salty wind of Colwyn Bay, where I used to
work.
Seagulls became my friend, Throwing Scraps of food from
my hotel window to you all, before going down to work to
serve breakfast.

Tables cleared; I could have a rest
before making guests' beds, and keeping rooms clean.
Was hard work, I didn't mind 17 was not as old then as now.

Oh, I miss my dear Wales as
much as I did then.
When the season ended,
all the guests gone,
home to Liverpool once again,
to brothers and sisters and I, made 10.
59 years old today, I went back
to Wales, for a holiday.
Llandudno up the road from Colwyn Bay, where I used to
work,

A Beautiful Hotel, Marine where my belly
is full, of the nicest food, from Wales,
the Waitress doing her very best to
make may stay happy. Nothing too much

trouble, as she carries my empty plates
away, tired she looks, but never complains,
A bed I sink into, comfortable and warm.
Sea views from the windows of spotless
Llandudno, Next day on one of our trips
coach drivers that risk their lives, as
they drive to slate mines high in the
mountains, where you can almost touch the
clouds.

A history lesson we have learnt of Miner's hell on earth,
But how can you learn, when it's all a rush,
2 hours just aren't enough.

The Seaside I Remember

Long days, serving guests at the Meadow Croft hotel, North Wales.
Making beds, cleaning rooms, to perfection.
Washing dishes, laying tables.
Hoovering crumbs from the floor,
One day off, too tired to enjoy the lovely
views of Colwyn Bay. And hear the seagulls!
Too tired to worry anymore.
Left home to find peace, but got none, did I dad,
You found me and brought all my sisters and brothers to see me.
I was doing fine until then.
Even though it was lovely to see all my
brothers and sisters.
My friend Betty had told you where I worked,
Why couldn't you leave me be, always controlling,
Trying to control me,
Working hard to build me reputation,
proud I come back home, but the cruelty started soon after,

I was sorry to be home.

Please Come With Me Away For A Break

I understand your problem, I'm sorry.

I'm patient as you know,

But wouldn't it be lovely,

If Italy we could go.

Can't you see I'm lonely for your company at times.

To share adventures and good times.

Just for once to have a nice time,

I can go away with friends,

But it wouldn't be the same,

I think it's sad and such a shame,

please can we have a break,

You refuse to go on holiday or even consider my request.

Please just for once, stop and think

can this relationship really last?

It's A New Day

Even though the sky is grey,
It's a new day, It's a new day
Recovery on its way after
Sadness and Health went down
It's a brand new day
let's see what the future
brings.

Let's sing a nice happy song.
What will it be,
So many to choose from
Lucky, Lucky me,
It's a brand new day,

One day things will get better.
Recovering from an illness
takes it out of you.
Slow steps rest and healthy food
And look after you.

A long road to recovery
but you'll get there in the end.
Be prepared for the depression
and feeling blue but that's normal, too.

You must have felt very tired
The illness did not come on its own
Working hard, all that stress and
Worry.
Now it's time to sit back Relax
and Nurture you. You deserve to be well.

It's <u>not</u> being selfish
It's helping you <u>Survive</u>, you have to
live too.

Too much running around after
others, has made you ill. Don't you agree.
So come on, be merry.
Eat for health. Get well.
And I'll drink to that
but only in moderation,
here's to you. Have a Happy Recovery!

It's A New Start

Moving house in the future
For peace that I crave
no use staying here
In end up in an early grave
Yes it can be stressful
Yes, it's hard to say goodbye
To friends you have made along
the years, and family that's made me
cry.
But sometimes, one gets weary,
of upsets and the blows.
And maybe if I move,
I'll feel better and it will show,
my health is falling here,
And I'm tired of all the noise

One day, things will be better,
And that's when I'll jump.
For joy, and have contentment.
I deserve that much you know.

My Poor Dear Friend

If I could heal your painful leg. An ulcer that has eaten your flesh I would!

If I could take away the hurt I would, if I could, I would!

You're my dear friend, my dear dear friend who cried when my breakdown nearly took my life,

Who made me laugh when we were at school together?

When we drank your dads' homemade wine and played Truant from the bullies at school.

I'm sorry, for all the years that have passed us by,

Not keeping in touch, when you live so close by,

I miss our friendship, but the years have changed you,

Why have you become so bitter?

I too have had bad times, lost a little girl, cot death 6 months old,

The day you came to visit me,

I tried to make it up to you for the pain and hurt you have suffered over the years. It hurt, you didn't write a little note to say Thank you,

But that's only bad manners on your part,

I won't turn my back, because I'll always remember the good times, I'll still keep in touch ask you how you are, maybe next time you'll make me as Welcome as I made you.

A Christmas Worry For Us All

Christmas a time to Relax, drink and eat, until our hearts content. Watch repeats on the telly, enjoy the Queen's speech. Open presents, admire the lights on the Christmas tree, tinsel and baubles but Christmas can be a sad time as well as a joyous occasion, loved ones gone. Missing from the arm chair.

Carols sung, beautifully, some sad, can shed a tear. Cards full of love with glitter and verses wishing a Happy Christmas and an even better New Year.

But I like others, find the build up to Christmas, a worry, every year expectations of the presents I've bought, hoping it's not disappointed faces I see, but every year, gets harder as I try to please and buy a little Gift.

Money rather scarce, we all have bills, so I look around charity shops, hoping to find a garment that's still got the tag on, new and not worn, for you to wear.

My mum says, why do you do it? When you haven't got the means, But! I say, rather too loud, it's just my way of saying

I love you, and it doesn't cost the earth. But this year, I have to work harder. Prices are going up, and up all the time and if I don't pay my bills, I'll come unstuck. You see, my nieces and my nephews, my granddaughters too, I don't always see them but how can I forget you?

Out of sight, out of mind, is not true, every day I worry Because I love …all of you, so my little gift and hard work is to say Merry Christmas with all my love,
I love you. X

Hungry Children

Bellies that growl out for food, swollen, hurting pain. Legs thin with Rickets, Hair, once long fall out, with hunger and lack of iron.

This can't be happening, can it? My child is suffering. Mum, I'm hungry! Her son cries but what can she do? Shall she steal to feed her child? The anxiety mounts please God help me! She prays. She has no Reply.

What did she expect, she had stopped praying years ago, his feet with shoes that no longer fit, paining him, Blisters, what could I do? Glued together to keep them from falling apart. I had to find a way to feed my son, and myself, but I would not, could not sell my body.

I decided I would write each day and send my stories off. After the second lot of short stories and poems, she got a reply, but the Publishers wanted money. I didn't have any, but I would not give up, I got a small job as a Housekeeper, in a private house, the money helped, we were no longer hungry.

My son grew into a fine well-educated man. But I am sure he often looks back at the childhood where he suffered, I am sorry but out of his suffering he has had success!

This short story says that men are important to me. I respect them. I have a lovely daughter, but I don't mention how she suffered too nor how I suffered. I was brought up by a dad and mum who always put a man first of "course man was born first." Adam and Eve but ladies are important too!

This Little Town

I never wanted to leave
this little Town I call home
but lately I've felt tired
And very much alone.

Not many friendly faces
when I need cheering up
Just bad news I keep hearing
men who no longer care
Moping around, drinking, drugs
women with weary faces
depressed, full of despair.
money short, shops expensive
You've gave up.
Just ghosts I see here.
Once a thriving place.
But sadly not anymore
I'll pass away quicker
if I stay here.
So please let me go.

Only A Little Mouse

A little mouse lives in a hole under the floorboards in my house. Forever eating and getting fat and running around. Bloated, I am sure he likes to scare me he makes a mess for me to clean his little feet runs quickly across the bedroom floor, squeak, squeak, he speaks, I throw a shoe, but miss, oh! If only he gave me a respite, please little mouse I shout I won't hurt you. Let me have some peace, you're running around all night. He never listens to me even when I shout.

Every day he gets fatter. His tail is long and frightens me. What can I do? It's his home too. Though he pays no rent. He's doing no harm, you say. He's only a little mouse. Yes, but he keeps me awake. Or is it worry that's keeps me awake?

Never mind little mouse I say, I can't keep feeding him as well. You can stay. Another lodger won't make much difference. After all, it's cold outside, and I'm not that cruel, am I, but please when you're gnawing your teeth little mouse, please keep the noise down and let me sleep. Squeak.

Goodbye Jack

Before I died, I said my prayers,
Forgive him God for all the years,
I thought he had moved on, from childish pranks at school.
He was always the one that broke the rules.

Jack my friend, and tormentor too.
What the hell, did I ever do to you?
You got me drunk.
Then pushed me over. I fell to cold and sea,
But I'll have the last laugh, Jack.

You saved me from taking my own life,
and it won't look so bad
So I might have died, revenge for you,
But Jack, I wanted to end it all anyway,
There is a bullet at the end of this cruise,
Waiting for you. A hitman too,
Goodbye Jack.

The Christmas Tree

6ft tall my Christmas Tree
Green Gold and Silver
Red tinsel draped around and around.
A Fairy sits with pride, a smile on
Her lovely Porcelain Face, Golden hair
and Paper Wings.
She's glad to be the center of
Attention.
Ginger Biscuits hang from each
Branch, tied with silk yellow Ribbons.
White lights twinkle in the Dark
As I listen to Christmas carols
Sung with love from a Welsh choir.
Presents wrapped brightly, some
big, some small, boxes for you all.
Round, Square, Long,
Hopefully with all the presents that you
wished for. Presents that I
can't afford. Not to worry, only
Kidding. They may be Second
Hand, but they're nice and
picked with thought and care.
Things have been tough this year.

Homemade bread in the Oven
Mulled Wine and Christmas
Pudding, Turkey, Mince Pies, Pigs
In Blankets. Roast Potatoes,
Yorkshire Puddings, Sprouts,
Carrot's Glazed. Then at last
We all sit back. Relax it's
Christmas with the chocs.

My Lovely Purple Thistle

A thistle scratches my lovely blue tartan skirt.
Pulling me back to where I belong, I'm to leave this home of mine, to go where ma Husband can find work.

Begone with your Scottish songs, which bring tears to my eyes, I hear the bagpipes in the distance, I'm sad to leave my home of Dalbeattie Scotland.

One day I will return, not too long, I hope. I walk through the woods, for one last time, bluebells cover the forest floor. My brothers and I played hide and seek as children here.
We caught rabbits, the Gamekeeper caught us once. I hid a ferret down my top in case he knew what we were doing in the woods. I was terrified in case the ferret bit me. Thank goodness he didn't.

Times were very hard back then, I say my goodbyes to childhood friends. One last look at the home I grew up in Sunny Side, I'm sad to leave.

A Good Cup Of Yorkshire Tea Please

A good cup of tea awaits me
A homemade scone with cream and
blackcurrant jam,
To fill my empty belly, it's 11 O'clock
What more could a girl ask.
No such luck, just wishful thinking.
I start the cleaning, bathroom first.
Don't you forget my dear to do the stairs.
The lady of the house gives her orders.
I wash and scrub, brush the floor
polish the silver.
Surely there's no more.
Everywhere is gleaming.
I hear the lady of the house.
Screaming down my ears from
stairs I'd cleaned.
Get up here, and finish the job,
If you don't, you're out.
I'd had enough, I'm not treated well.
Go to hell I shout back
you horrible old Bat.

A Chill In My Bones

God, I feel cold, from the chill from my wife, she 'seems' a bit down of late. Never wants to hold me anymore. No affection, I know I don't take her out. Never buy flowers. Is it because I take her for granted? The last flowers I got her were free from the graveyard. The food she serves me is not fit for a dog, but she tries, poor dear she tries. Could be because I don't take her out. I just can't be bothered making the effort anymore, why should I bother, she's ugly. She's put on so much weight, her hair's gone grey, she's really let herself go. Double chins, she's such a sight. Nevermind, if she is good tonight, I might let her watch the television. After all, she hasn't been very well lately. I wonder if her best friend is coming over, she's a real dishy lady, I fancy her rotten. Better looker than the wife. Maybe I'll go on the computer and get a date from the Hearts channel. You never know I might meet someone else. It's been two weeks since I got on the computer. I've had I reply. Janet, but she knew me from years ago. "You're a married man, does your wife know you're using date chat up lines?" she said. I didn't reply to her, oh well it's back to the old bat of a wife. Can't understand why I only got one reply.

After all, I'm a good catch, and a handsome devil.

I Lost My Job Today

I lost my job today,
I've had to walk away,
Pay was bad, yes I'm sad.
But never worked out for me.
I walk on home, I need some air
What can I tell her, the wife?
I call in my local, for a pint.
It might deaden the feelings of flight.
I've not much left in the bank to pay my way.
But bills can't be left unpaid I say.
I turn around to see a friend.
John my old mate from school.
Nearly 30 years ago, he hasn't changed
Just a little fatter.
He's still the friendly lad I knew
How are you? I hear him say
I lost my job John today
I buy him a pint to break the ice
I can't believe I've walked out of my job.
But it was hell.
Good for you I hear him say.
You've been true to yourself.
Thanks, I say, and feel better.

School Bully

Throwing screwed paper that hits me
on my head.
You pull at my pig tails
I wish that you were dead
The School Bully that you are
I try hard to listen to the Teacher
It's a subject that I like Religion Instruction
How can I study when I am the subject
of your hate.

I've asked my god, to forgive me
for all my evil thoughts,
but I really hate you and can't
forgive you.
I've tried to understand you.
I believe you've had it tough
But I am tired of excuses.
You're too rough for me.
At first I felt sorry, but feeling
Sorry's not enough
You're just an insecure Bully
and you're not that tough.

Today I told the Teacher, couldn't
Keep it inside no more
Fed up feeling frightened and
going out my door.
Maybe there will be repercussions
of that, I just don't care.
I can't be ruled by a Bully
Year after year,
I'm glad I told the Teacher.

My Garden Of Peace

The peace I have is when I hear the gentle wind,
Blowing through the Blackcurrant Bush
Berries almost ripe to pick and eat.
I am looking forward to that treat.
I watch Her Majesty my chicken golden red and full
of Pride, eating insects walking on the soil.
It's said they're still alive when the chickens eat them,
Mrs Duck walking through the overgrown grass
that soon will have to be cut.
Quacking, to let me know, Mum I'm here, I'm fine,
My other little chicken, who very nearly died.
A Battery Hen when I first got her.
She's suffered in her time.
Caught a cold last winter, but thank God
she's survived by eating garlic and drinking
Cider vinegar, she's still here, by my side.
Timmy my sheep dog, waiting patiently for me to
throw his ball, glaring at me with his lovely brown eyes,
He'll have to wait a little longer.
I need a good strong cup of Yorkshire tea
A Ginger nut, to dip. Time to relax and write my story
Then I can get back to you all.

Jay a friend to Timmy. What a lovely dog she is
she's a friend to all the pets, who'd think she went
hungry at one time, thrown out because she was
moulting on the carpet and made a mess
how can people be so cruel.
I took her in, Company for Timmy
And myself.
My wonderful little family keep
Me so busy.
And the Turtles make me smile, Jimmy
And Jamie, they both enjoy the telly
It's almost time to end the day
I say thank you to the lovely Black
Bird, who has sung for me all day.
I throw an apple for his Tea.
I hope he enjoys it, he flies down,
Thanks little family, everyone of
You, Personalities you all have
Unique and wonderful in your
Own little ways.
Timmy rounds up the Duck and
Chickens. They sit in the outhouse on straw
As they come in the door
I feel blessed and happy
With them all. Night, Night
I say to them, And they all rest.

Behind Closed Doors I Hide

I hide away behind net curtains watching the world go by.
Happy not to join in with all the rushing about. Cup of tea
down here, My Partner shouts. Okay, I will be down in a
minute. I feel a wave of depression come over me.

My granddaughter has guest been beaten up by her Ex-
Partner. He broke into her house at 7 in the morning, by
smashing her window, her little baby besides her. I feel sick,
to think of the fear and fright she must of went through, my
lovely Granddaughter of 19 years old.

Today I feel vulnerable. It has brought back bad memories of
the violence I have been through. Are all man like this I
wonder. My dad was violent, my children's father violent, my
daughter's ex-partner, and now this my granddaughter's
partner. What triggers violence, it is there a bringing?
Four ladies have been murdered where I live, what an earth is
happening?

Counting the minutes

The clock in the corner, says 1/4 to 9
I am counting every minute until home time.
I've got terrible backache with this old wooden chair
I am starting to feel hungry.
And I am dying of thirst
Tick, Tock, Tick, Tock,
slowly the minutes pass,
There's so much to do.
In so little time.
Books to Mark
Pupils to learn.
I am giving a History Lesson
on Rome and the Roads the
Romans built. Interesting stuff but
some are falling asleep
no wonder with empty bellies
malnutrition, rotten teeth
shoes glued together, falling off
their feet.
I try to tell their parents
But half look malnourished too.
It's best to say nothing,
But sometimes nothing doesn't do.

I'm watching and waiting the minutes
Going by.
BRR, BRR, BRR, The bell rings at
Last.
Kids run through the door
It's another day over,
I'm weary and I'm tired,
When I look back.
I'm glad that I'm retired.
Being a Teacher was no fun at all,
Boy I'm glad I headed out that door.

I'd Name It Carl After You

If I could pluck a star from the Heavens.
The biggest one would only do.
I'd pick the brightest one and pass it on to you.
Star Carl Anthony your lovely name.
I'd want nothing in return
but a great big smile would do.

You gave me all I could ever want.
I gave nothing in return
you see I have lovely memories
and those memories are of you.
Carl Anthony my son who I've
never heard complain.

Do you remember as a little boy
you used to help me cook the tea.
Sausage rolls, and gingerbread men
when you were only three.
You'd run and hide behind the garden shed,
And laugh at my despair and fright,
tears running down my face until I found you.

One day you said,
"I'm hungry mum."
There was nothing there to eat.
You never complained when we
walked miles in the snow to
deliver newspapers to the rich.
You used to share your wages with me,
very little money too.
It helped to feed your sister, dad and I. And Biddy
our Jack Russell.
You never once complained, not once.

We all had terrible bad times back then.
You were always strong, never ever weak.
Christmas time I could never buy you the latest toys,
but you never complained not once,
when the toys were bought so cheap.

Today you're a success, tall and handsome,
with a wife and child, Isabella. You'll never be a loser, Carl!
And I am sorry it's been tough growing up.
I understand it only too well.
But hey! Look at you today.
You owe me not a thing.
But it would be good sometimes to hear you moan.
Be music to my ears.
Then I can listen and repay my debt to you,
and sing I love you.

The Dentist Chair

"Open wide!" The Dentist says with a smile.

I don't like him. My first impression. Can't he see how terrified I am? His hands are so hairy. He bites his nails, he is ugly.

"Oh yes! that tooth is beyond repair Mrs. Gee,"

Please God don't let me die.

"I think the tooth must come out I'm afraid! Mrs. Gee."

Afraid, afraid, he says, it's me who is rooted to the chair afraid! But I can't understand why. His breathe smells, food sticking to his beard.

"Just a slight sting in your gum it won't hurt."

Is the needle clean, I think and yes, it does hurt! It's stinging. The pain shoots right up to my head, such a thick needle. Tears trickle down my cheek. It felt like I had a swarm of wasps, inside my mouth.

"There, there, Mrs. Gee, that wasn't too bad, was it?"

Yes, it was! I think.

"In just a few minutes I will take the bad decayed tooth out."

"Please Sir I say, don't let me swallow the tooth, I want a promise."

But I feel I can't trust him, his white overall is grubby, his shoes not polished, his hair and beard unkept, and when he opens his mouth to speak, I see he has a few gravestones for teeth of his own. I'm sorry I came to this dentist I really am, I think. My gum feels numb, I feel dizzy, I am going to faint. Oh, please God, get me out of here in one piece.

"Mrs. Gee you're shaking, don't worry Mrs. Gee, it's just your nerves."

My head feels like it's been in a vice. I hate him, he's a horrible man, even the light over the Dentist chair is full of dead flies.

It's filthy, why hasn't it been cleaned, I want to shout, to scream, but the instruments are going in deep pulling, tugging. It seems like forever, my mouth hurts. As soon as he takes his instruments out of my mouth, I let out a scream.

"Mrs. Gee! Mrs. Gee! Calm down, it's all over. We've got the tooth out."

I rinse my blooded mouth out. I feel I've been punched by a Boxer.

He speaks, "Mrs. Gee, we will take the other bad tooth out at the next appointment."

"WHAT!" I say.

"Ah yes! he says, one more tooth needs to come out, its rotten."

I shakily head out the door, blood pouring from my mouth, my legs like jelly. I'm Nearly out the door leading to fresh air, freedom, when I hear him shout, after me. What does he want?

"Mrs. Gee, Mrs. Gee"

Oh God, leave me alone. I just want to get home.

"I've just looked at your Xray, Mrs. Gee. I am so, so very sorry, I've taken the wrong tooth out."

The End

You're Beaten

Hey, man shooting bullets You've missed.
Are you pissed?
Is that a toy gun you use?
Maybe you need glasses.
Mine where free.
Down! Your weapons drop them to the floor!
Time to give up, and fight no more.
Accept you're beaten.
At least you tried.
But hey, we're the SAS, the best,
what did you expect.
We wear our badge with pride.
We know our stuff;
you won't get the better of us.
Nothing gets in our way.
Stand up straight! You piece of ….
Do you hear what I've to say?
You waved a white flag, or could it be
a bloodied rag. You've made my day,
You've blood on your hands.
Let's take you away.
Time to say goodbye, you ugly runt.
You've got my Mens death, on your dirty hands.

No dirty washing in their back yards
What you crying for? You piece of ….
It is guilt or shame?
There's only yourselves to blame,
Are you laughing?
It's been a long day for me.
Don't push my buttons! You're not free.
I've had enough of this heat.
Sweat running down to my exhausted feet,
and bones.
You look ill man! Who's laughing now?
Missing your mummy's arms?
Didn't she feed you? You've scrawny arms,
fluff for a beard. Was she a cow?
You're not a real man. Just a kid.
I'm the SAS. Have you heard of us?
Trained to sort out problems.
Trained to kill.
Press my buttons, I'm in control
unlike you.
You're just a savage, cuts heads to kill.
You hide behind your mask
A coward in disguise.
Just give me one reason
Why I don't shoot you, between the
eyes. Yes, you need glasses, you've a squint
But why waste a bullet,
On scum like you. They cost money
and in England, it's cutbacks too.
I'm in the SAS, I'm proud and true.
I'm in control, not you anymore.

you can't even control your piss.
So, get moving faster, you
skinny little runt. Or I'll flatten
your face on her floor
away from your mummy.
Her tears and cries.
I'm the man who has all the
ties. To sort the likes of you
No more connections for you.

A Beautiful Garden

My friend Joan had invited me to lunch in Kirby, where she lives.

The journey was long.

The bus was old.

The driver was grumpy, he was late I am told, please slow down! Not to worry I'm almost there, factories and fresh air.

I enjoy the sights of Knowsley. Farms and people going about up there, little houses on the way.

The hour soon passes by and she's there to meet me off the bus. A smile greeted me, so warm. She is such a lovely girl, but I am feeling grumpy, the journey lacked comfort. The driver was a bore. I feel a little rough.

"Never mind sitting in a cafe, let's go to mine," she says loud, I'm pleased she says this, my purse feels a little light, and empty. A cup of tea at £1.00 is quite a lot to spend.

Half an hour later, a lovely house I see, "oh Joan, it's lovely!"

"That's mine," she says.

Without bragging.

But if it was mine, I'd brag you see.

We sat in a beautiful garden. This is heaven, I think. No, it is not heaven, but Brian's hard work and toil and Joan's nice chap, he's friendly as long as he's good to Joan.

I munch on homemade butties of beetroot, meat and feel warm, content, happy to see my friend.

After a chat, two cups of coffee I need to move quite quickly, my bus in half an hour and it is quite a trip.

We say our goodbyes, arrange to see her again.

I've all these lovely memories of her garden, summer, and her good man, I'll treasure, of my lovely school friend, who found me after all.

It's Never Too Late

WEARY BACKS, WEARY MEN,

Going down the mines, coal dust, shit lying on your lungs,
cold, damp, backs breaking when the day was over, finally,
exhausted with worry, pain, glad to get out of the pit, going
home to homemade Welsh Cakes, not much of fruit in them,
"Cage Bach"
Have you forgotten them?
It's never too late to make amends to the miners our forgotten
men.

Orange Marigolds

Marigolds
Rich orange bold and bright,
Lights up my garden with colour and delight,
distracts me from the clutter that surrounds me.

Like a desert sun going down at night
And sand pits when I was a child.
Empty dreams of long ago,
how young I was, back then
not much left have I to show but
memories coloured by LSD is what the Doctor gave
to me, please take me back when I was free
I was called a Nutter and hospitalised
but that's OK, I didn't mind.

Pink blanket on my bed
Softens blows of brothers dead
Pink and pretty, pale like I
laying in the gutter cold and bleeding
why did they, have to die?
Three brothers gone,
No longer breathing.

White painted rooms to make them
look bigger, my house is small, as I,
white Roses for you my lovely brother
that you no longer smell,

Green light to say what I can cross
upon that dangerous road, page moss,
Green leaves, a blade of grass
all these memories of my past
my little shoes the colour of a frog
where is my prince now?
He has gone, into the past.

Black clouds over head
Will it rain when I am passed.
Black boots to march along
Roman Roads, they sing their songs.

Red for danger, Red for broken hearts
Red when lovers part, Anger, Tears, and
Grief, a long and lonely time to bear.

Yellow days of summer June
Pretty flowers bloom
A cup of tea makes it all worthwhile
Yes please, I say with a smile.

The end

The Blues

The terrible blues, of yesterday
that never go away
always there
they get in my way
obstacles I've been through
I call them the Gray.
I dreamt last night.
I was put away,
and I felt frightened and confused
I was in a hospital. Where am I?
Rain Hill Hospital you said to me
Feeling very very ill.
Felt much better after Doctor gave
me a pill, three months inside.
If you don't shut up.
I heard a nurse shout to me
I'll put you in a Straight Jacket
she was a night nurse.
Not much patience with me.
I was chatting, I was on the mend

Putting My Feet Up No Chance

No rest for the wicked, that's what I was told. God finds work
for idle hands my Ninny said, when she grew old.
Can't I have a rest then?
Will it always be hand Graft.
Very little cash then?
I answer back,
I'm tired of being poor Nin.
It's no picnic down here too, many worries,
And I don't drink beer to blot it all out
Can you hear me Nin in heaven I shout, she doesn't answer
back.
I can't repay her
For all she done
For me,
She used to curl my hair
And sit me on her knee
I guess I was the favourite
She bought me nice clothes
Made me egg and bacon on her
broken down old stove
Even shared her scone, always gave me half
But life with its twists
And turns, took her in the dark

To my Nin away, a Stroke
At the age of 73
Not that old, was she
But life had dealt her
A lousy pack of cards
She struggled until she died
I'm sorry Nin it was not to be
A very happy life
Cleanliness is next to godliness
She used to say to me
Moving fast forward
I'm lying here in bed
Thinking of all the lovely
Things that she ever said,
"One day Pearl you'll be happy"
"You'll marry a millionaire He'll adore you and curl
Your lovely red hair"
It was not to be
I was married twice
But Nin, One made me happy
The other put me in a vice
But not to worry Nin
Two were not that nice.
I've met another man
Two years younger
He does what he can for me.
No we're not married
Well, I'll have to wait and see,
Yes and life has been a struggle,
But God's been good to me.
So Nin, please don't worry

Even though you are up there in the clouds,
One day things will get better,
But I'll have to do more graft.
Time stands still for no man
I'm tired of watching my back
Hard work never killed anyone
Well I hope it never kills me.
Because I'll keep on writing
What I feel, until I say
Goodbye to thee!

The End

Humbugs for Christmas

Pauline my private nurse, puts my best pyjamas onto me, she's an angel. I have to look presentable for when I meet my maker. Who, ever he'll be, God or Devil. I'm too ill, to help, the end is creeping up at last. Pauline puts water to my lips into my tired old, neglected body, it runs down I no longer take any food, too painful for me, she whispers to my son, who sits by the bed,

"He won't last the night."

She thinks I can't hear her say this, but I can. I'm not quite ready yet Pauline! I want to say, but I'm too weak, too tired, too exhausted.

My son can't wait, he fidgets with his watch, I suppose my other child can't wait too. He's already spent too much time by my side, the other daughter visits me hardly ever.

I'll come back in the morning then.

Jeffry says to Pauline.

When it's all over.

Pauline looks shocked but says nothing.

Jeffry come back I love you! I'm sorry!

But the words won't come out, I want to say to him.

I drift in and out of a drug induced sleep the hours loudly ticking away on the Grand Father clock, 6 o'clock, it's morning I wake up I've made it through the night, I'm cold, Pauline snores, her head resting on her chest, she's fast asleep. Why is she fast asleep?

Why is she not awake, wake up Heather!

I pay her enough, the anger I feel is soon replaced with acceptance, she's exhausted, but so am I. I treated her badly. I hated her too.

Sunlight floods through the open thick velvet red drapes. They cost a small fortune. I see flecks of snow fakes falling past the unwashed windows. The maid who cleaned them has long since left. Who could blame her. I treated her badly too.

They put too much on my shoulders. Far too much pressure, want, want, want over the years. I worked 12-hour days to provide them with every comfort I could afford. Luxury holidays, clothes, spending money, but even though my wife wanted for nothing, she left me for another man, that was 40 years ago, I changed after that, I became bitter angry and full of hate. I could no longer trust any woman, not even my two daughters, Heather and Daisy.

Heather: tall beautiful, the image of her mum, dark long curly hair. We never got on. Reminded me of her mother too much. Daisy: short, fat, nothing to rave about, but had a bubbling personality, she was different in so many ways than Heather, she was caring, and kind was my Daisy. She took her own life, was I to blame? In a lot of ways yes, I treated my family rotten, horrible, nasty me. I started to resent them all, resent is too nice a word, I grew to hate them! At first, in the beginning I was happily married at 26 to a beautiful wife, 2 daughters came along and then a son. I thought my life was happy, she had everything. I thought we were the perfect family. I only hit her 6 times. Why did she spoil it all?

Why did I let my insecurity ruin everything, it all went back to my childhood, lots of sisters, I was the only boy, I got pushed out being the oldest child, I had all the responsibility when my father passed away with T.B.

My sisters never spoilt me, I had to be the man of the house, I had to take the worry on my thin shoulders to provide for them all, that's what a man did. I didn't want them to have the worry, but that worry was passed to me! I got myself a job, worked my way up in a Humbug factory, ha ha I've still got a sense of humour, even when I's dying.

The Factory was small, but popular. We made sweets, we did well with the Humbugs. Humbugs were my favourite.

Christmas time I hated giving the workers Christmas holidays, they all wanted something from me, I hated them all, I gave them packets of Humbugs, but I must admit they did work hard, though I did catch one or two stealing the sweets over Christmas and filling their mouths with my profits.

It was all so long ago, I an old man surely my maker will forgive me, I hear the doorbell, Pauline jumps up, answers it, then my son walks into the room, he looks angry, he sounds angry. Not dead yet! He says to Pauline who's been woken up and not too pleased.

"For god's sake, how can you talk about your dad like that?" she shouted.
I forgot to mention my son's name didn't I, "Jeffry", silly old Jeffry.

My son shouts back, "Know your place!" he says to Pauline, "You're only the hired help!"

Pauline sticking up for me, maybe she cares more than I thought she did. Jeffry hated the name I gave him, but who cares, I hated him, the wimp. Never done a hard day's work in his entire life. But I'm a writer Dad! He used to say.
A writer, he couldn't even spell his name until he was 16, and he can't spell.
What do you write about Jeffry?
I write poems, ha ha, should have heard some of the crap he wrote. But I used to humour him and pretend to understand what he wrote. It was all a load of dribble if you asked me.
After all no one had ever paid him for his stupid poems.
No one wanted to publish them, they were that bad.
So who kept Jeffry in clothes, food, roof over his baldy head? Me! Me! Me! I was drained for years, thank goodness the sweet factory was doing well, I worked until midnight. Sometimes I felt so tired. I wondered who I could rely on if I got ill. No one! No one! No one! I had to be strong to provide my wife spending on luxuries jewelry, clothes, but I loved her, she was my world. At first I didn't notice, but I felt pushed aside by my wife and the spending didn't stop, it got worse.

One day on a rare day off, I snapped, I was exhausted. I had a funny turn at the factory and fainted, no fuss was made, by my staff, smelling salts brought me around, I think my staff were wishing I was dead.

My health was starting to suffer, my wife Isabelle didn't show me any concern. No understanding, no empathy, no tender loving care for me, I hit her, blacked her eye, she was so hard towards me, yes, I'd been rotten to her and the children growing up but I was under so much stress at the factory.

Half the staff wouldn't turn up, in the holidays, Easter, Christmas, once excuse after another, eating my Humbugs all day stuffing their mouths with gossip, and their pockets with my sweets what did they want from me? I'm an old man, I'm not well. My daughter's death was such a terrible shock, found her in the stables, hung herself, left a suicide note, it read like this.

"I can't take anymore; I hate working at the Factory. Dad, I get bullied because I'm the boss's daughter, I'm fat and ugly. No one could love me, you don't love me, they call me the ugly duckling in work, you don't pay me, I work for nothing, I feel trapped at home. Trapped and unhappy, I don't have any money to leave, where would I go? Even you Dad, call me names. Why do you say to me,

"You're fat my Dear!" No one wants to cuddle and, that double chin with all my Humbugs you eat, at the factory. You haven't even got a good set of teeth, bad with eating sweets. I'd be better off dead.

Bye Bye Dad and Mum, I hope Dad you rot in hell."

Why! Why! Why! Did she do this to me? I always told her when I died, she'd get plenty of money, my house and lands. That's why I never gave her a wage. Such a shame, a waste. With a good diet, a new set of teeth, a new hairdo, could have worked wonders on her. It wasn't down to me, she was born so ugly, of course Isabelle blamed me, they all blamed me. Why could no one understand what I had done to provide for them all. 12-hour days, hardly any holidays year after year at the Factory to provide all the luxuries they enjoyed what about me?

A knock as loud as thunder wakes me from the memories of the past.

It's Doctor Death, that's his real surname, honestly.

He enters the bedroom.

Hello Issac, he says loudly like thunder, comes over to my right side, takes my pulse with his long boney fingers and smiles, with his thin lips and sunken eyes, bad teeth and yellow skin, he looks like death himself. Why is he smiling? and rubbing his hands? Oh yes, I remember to keep in his good books, I promised him some land, if I should die, no wonder he's rubbing his dirty grubby hands. I'm giving you some more pain relief Issac! He says with a sly grin. I don't want more! Go away! But I can't speak, I'm too tired! I've even had to work for the pain relief, you get nothing for nothing, I've suffered for the morphine he gave me, might as well enjoy it, I drift off, cost me enough.

Jeffry's big mouth awakens me, he's shaking me. Don't die Dad! What, what, what's he on about? I'm not dead yet, but I can't speak, I open my eyes.

What is he crying for?

Oh Dad! We love you, don't die!

He's such a wimp!

It's not me he loves, it's been my money, sponging off me all these years.

Leave me alone Jeffry, If I was well, I'd put your head in a headlock and beat you with the Cane, like I used to do until you're black and blue. Get away from me, I hate your guts and always have!

I glare at him, such a wimp. We all die, my time is nearly up. I've peed my underclothes. The bed is soaking wet. Where is that girl? Pauline, she doesn't deserve a wage.

I've got bed sores, I'm thirsty, where is that horrible girl?

At last, here she is, my eyes glare at her, she ignores me. I think you've had a little accident, Issac. The bed is soaking wet.

Forget the bed, I'm soaking wet you stupid woman. I'm cold, but I'm too tired and ill to say what I want, I can only glare at her.

I'm cold, I'm dying, but I can still hear and see, I still feel discomfort, Doctor Death still here, I can hear him talking to good old Jeffry on the landing, he shouts when he talks, always did have a big mouth, makes up for his lack of height I suppose.

Issac's very, very ill. He won't last the week, has he got his affairs all in order Jeffry? Dr Death shouts.

I know of a good Undertaker, he doesn't charge much, we can hurry things along oh my God! I hear every word, I'll haunt them all, every one of them will suffer, when I die.

What have I done in this life that is so bad, that they want to finish me off.

I made my Will as soon as I became ill with Cancer in my lungs, they'd all have a wonderful time, I'd looked after my Son, Daughter, Maid and Nurse Pauline oh and let's not forget the good old Doctor Death, they all had over the years plenty of my hard earned cash to spend on holidays and luxuries, houses, cars, clothes. Yes, I have looked after them all very, very well.

I'd go to my Maker when I decided, not Doctor Death or my Son.

I am just skin and bone, the pain is horrible. But no way is it as bad as the pain the family have caused me. Every one of them has feathered their nests, with my money. I had never drunk, never smoked, very seldom bought new clothes, my shoes had been glued together over and over, I am on my death bed, and I wear thread bare patched up old and wash out PJ's. My beard is out of control, but I would never cut it, same with my hair up to my shoulder, grey brittle greasy, hangs lankily. I punished myself to give to my family, I have neglected myself with food, eating very little, not finding time to rest, so much worry that had I on my shoulders. Yes, I'd be glad when it was all over, soon I'd be dead, out of pain, but I would not leave this earth just yet!

I never received any presents from my staff or children at Christmas that hurt me, not even a Christmas card, not even a Humbug. Christmas is only days away, yet I dreaded the Carol Singers every year who sang at the door. Why couldn't they sing a Christmas song, without wanting payment of some sort, Pauline gives me Humbugs.

They too wanted something from me, yet their voices where shrill, even the birds that knocked on my window with cold winter beaks, wanted food from my pantry, when all I ate was crumbs.

Jeffry and Heather trying to be nice to me in the run up to Christmas. It was my money they wanted but they never wanted me!

My feelings had long since died for Heather, she didn't act like a daughter. She was false, never came to see me, even when I'm ill, she doesn't cross the door, she's dead to me now.

Pauline's the only one really that has stuck around, but she too wants something from me for being cruel to her all these years, money after all, she had nothing but poverty, before she came to work for me 20 years ago. I still had control over who got my money. Not Jeffry, not Pauline, not Heather and certainly not Dr Death. That would be a lovely surprise for them when the Will was read.

I'm exhausted! I need some peace, Christmas Eve, I'm still alive, but only just.

Pauline, Jeffry, Dr Death all hanging around my bed. The pain I feel in my heart.

Pauline speaks first with lack of emotion,
It's snowing again Issac, it's very cold outside. She means, she's cold. Why Isn't the fire lit? Why is the window wide open? To answer my unspoken words Pauline says, fresh air, it's stuffy in here Issac. But I'm freezing! She's wrapped up, thick brown woolen coat, red scarf, I've only got thin cotton P.J's on, and cotton sheets, bed's wet. No hot water bottle, no woolen blankets, no fire in the grate. Do they hate me that much? Yes, it seems they do. Everything has been begrudged me. Even happiness, love, gentleness.

They wanted me to suffer, and I have suffered. Yet I gave them sweat, hard work, money, luxuries, and lastly my health. Even though I'd been cruel and unkind, life had been unkind to me too. I was ready to meet my Maker, I wanted peace.

I never did pray but I asked God to forgive me. To forgive the vultures around my bed, Hell was better than this life. In my Will I'd left them something sweet, they could remember me by, they could enjoy tomorrow Christmas Day. After all, it as "Humbugs!" that gave them luxuries, and I left in my Will a packet of my best Humbugs too each one of them, Pauline, Jeffry and Dr Death.

All my land, my house, my factory, everything I owned I left to the dog's home. I gave the dogs home everything! After all a dog is a man's best friend. And the only friend I ever had, was Bruce my little mongrel dog who was loyal, faithful to me when I was a child. He never asked for anything but gave me his love, his barking, his licking my face, Bruce, I'll see you soon.

I breathe my last Goodbye, Humbugs on Christmas Day to you all!

The End

Peace at Last, oh and yes, a packet of Humbugs to the ex-wife and the daughter who never came to see me.

Can't Keep Me Down For Long

Looking after my pennies,

Adds up to, not much at all

But pennies from heaven count

a bit more when I read my Bible

and I say my Prayers, Sometimes I

wonder do I offer you enough

a price to pay to listen Sir?

Jesus I wonder

Will I go to Heaven?

or will it be Hell?

Who's to tell?

I Could Do With A Helping Hand

Let me climb aboard, for god's sake
I feel like I'm going to drown
Oh look at that beautiful sky, oh man
I scream, as loud as I can, Lord
Help me, I scream again,
I don't want to die

I've always been strong
No one hears me,
I can feel my strength slipping away,
The water's freezing, my legs and arms feel numb
I'm clinging on to some driftwood, I'm so tired man

I don't understand, my life flashes before me,
I don't want to die
I think of my wife and son,
Little Dan, he's only 4
Why has it come to this?

I needed this holiday, needed the break
My work's quite stressful,
Teachers pay, never covers the costs

Of the ups and downs,
The students are distracted
When the teacher's not around.

My summer holidays at last
Were here, I was all packed, excited, ready to go
Planned a cruise trip,
To the Caribbean, as far away as possible
Jack and I, my mate from
School, and hell, used to hit me with school bell
Pity I played the fool,
He was always jealous of me, even then.

The wife she said, you go
Ahead
Enjoy your summers break
With Jack instead,
I'm not one, for the sun,
I'll stay here, get the garden
Done, I'll watch my flowers bloom.

After much persuasion
This is what I've done,
Gone on a cruise without her
Sweet Jesus,
I can't hang on
Can't breathe, I'm cold,
Why did Jack throw me over?